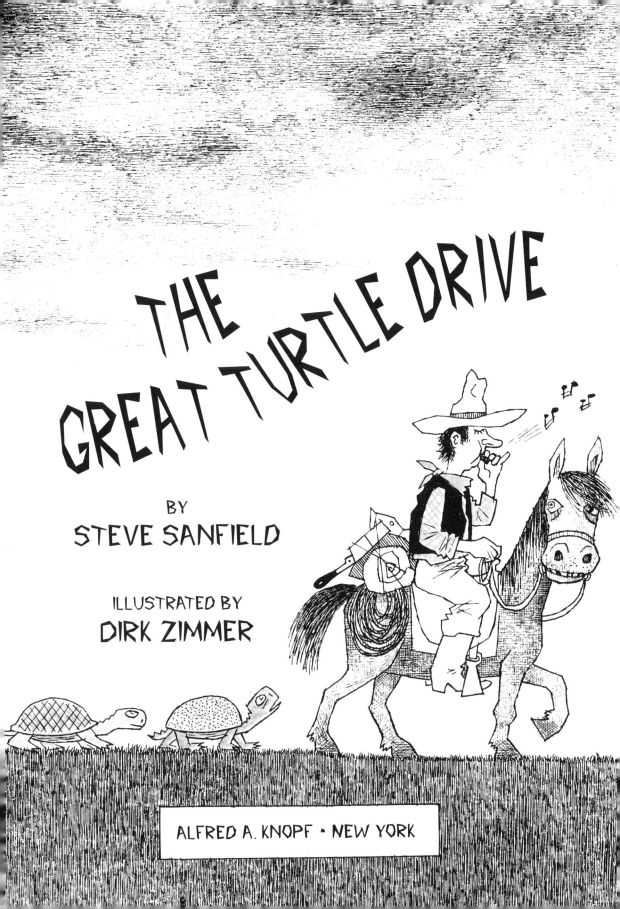

THE GREAT TURTLE DRIVE

BY
STEVE SANFIELD

ILLUSTRATED BY
DIRK ZIMMER

ALFRED A. KNOPF · NEW YORK

To Bob, Gay, Patrick, Susan,
comrades on the trail
— S. S.

To Cesar Matthies-Westphal
— D. Z.

THIS IS A BORZOI BOOK PUBLISHED BY ALFRED A. KNOPF, INC.

Text copyright © 1996 by Steve Sanfield
Illustrations copyright © 1996 by Dirk Zimmer

Library of Congress Cataloging-in-Publication Data
Sanfield, Steve.
The great turtle drive / by Steve Sanfield ; illustrated by Dirk Zimmer.
p.   cm.
Summary: When he sees how much a bowl of turtle soup costs, a cowboy comes up with an unusual plan to earn a fortune.
ISBN 0-679-85834-2 (trade) — ISBN 0-679-95834-7 (lib. bdg.)
[1. Turtles—Fiction. 2. Cowboys—Fiction. 3. Humorous stories.]
I. Zimmer, Dirk, ill. II. Title.
PZ7.S2237Gr   1995
[E]—dc20   93-43753

Manufactured in the United States of America
10 9 8 7 6 5 4 3 2 1

Want to hear a true story about how I made and lost a million dollars before I was old enough to vote? That's right, a million dollars.

When I was a young man, I was a true son of the Old West—from the peak of my ten-gallon hat right down to the tips of my pointy-toed boots. I was a cowboy and proud of it.

I used to work on those long cattle drives from west Texas up to Kansas City. We'd be on the trail with thousands of cows for two, sometimes three, months, and by the end you couldn't tell who smelled worse— us or the cows.

After we got paid and cleaned up, I always liked to eat a fine meal, so I'd go to my favorite restaurant, a fancy place

called Frenchy's Gourmet Eating Establishment and
Pizza Parlor.

This one time, I picked up the menu and it said SPECIAL OF THE DAY—TURTLE SOUP. Thinking I'd be a bit adventuresome, I ordered a bowl.

The waiter brought me this teeny tiny bowl of thick green soup. Not only was it delicious, but it was incredibly filling. I'd planned to order a seven- or eight-pound steak and maybe a raspberry pizza, but there just wasn't room for a single bite more.

I asked for the bill, and it said TURTLE SOUP—$4.00.

Four dollars?! That was an awful lot for a teeny tiny bowl of soup! "Waiter," I asked, "how many turtles does it take to make a bowl of turtle soup?"

"Sir," he said in that snooty waiter tone, "I believe it takes one turtle to make one bowl of turtle soup."

It was right then and there I got the idea that would turn me into a millionaire. Why couldn't *I* supply Frenchy with his soup turtles? He must be paying someone at least two dollars a turtle, and I figured that someone might as well be me.

You see, in Texas we've got turtles—we call them tortoises or land turtles—coming out the gooch, wherever the gooch is. You can't walk down a west Texas road at sunrise without seeing dozens of them crossing every which way, as if they were sharing the news.

So when I got back home, I began to round up turtles.

I tricked 'em,

I trapped 'em,

I lassoed 'em,

I netted 'em.

I even caught 'em with my bare hands—until by spring I'd collected the largest herd of turtles on the hoof—or, I should say, flipper—that had ever been assembled. I had a herd of 20,000 turtles.

Next, I went to some of my fellow cowpokes and asked, "You boys want to join me on a turtle drive?"

They looked at me. They looked at my turtles. They looked at each other. And then they walked away without saying a word. I guess none of them shared my vision.

So early one May morning, I set out alone—just me and my herd of 20,000 turtles.

Right away I knew it was going to be a long journey. We were only making 85 or 90 yards a day. It took us four days just to get out of the corral.

After about a week on the trail, I discovered I had a little problem. My turtles insisted on acting like cows. When we stopped, they wanted to wander off in all directions. To hold them together, I had to keep circling them, around and around all night long.

After two weeks, I was so worn out I could barely whistle a cowboy tune. After three weeks, I couldn't keep my eyes open. I'd fall asleep in the saddle and slide to the ground, landing on my elbows, or my knees, or my butt, or sometimes my head. Before long I was nothing but a bundle of bruises.

Something had to be done, and I did it. Each day I'd stop well before the sun went down and turn every last one of those turtles onto their backs. Now they'd spend

most of the night lying there, waving their flippers in the air as if they were singing church songs. That made *them* a little tired, but at least *I* was getting my rest.

It wasn't long before another small problem presented itself. All that walking made the turtles' flippers sore. What was needed were some horseshoes—or, I should say, turtle shoes. I stopped outside a town, turned them over so they'd stay put, and went in search of a blacksmith.

"I've got a herd of 20,000 turtles out there," I told him, "and their feet are mighty sore. Can you shoe them?"

"Sure, I can. Let's see, four shoes per turtle at ten cents a shoe...that'll be eight thousand dollars."

Of course, I didn't have enough money to do that, so instead I bought a few kegs of paper clips—extra-large paper clips. Then I gently slid one on each and every flipper.

That was a major improvement, and once my turtles got used to them, we really began to move. We were making one, sometimes two, miles a day, unless the wind was ahead of us. But it was still a long way to Kansas City.

We were out there on the High Plains when winter began to announce itself.

I knew if my turtles were exposed to that bitter cold and ice and snow, they'd all freeze to death. Once again something had to be done and I did it.

With the few dollars I had left, I hired a farmer to plow a deep trench in the sand. Then I drove my herd in and buried them, figuring they'd hibernate through the winter.

When I dug them up that spring, I was in for a big surprise. My herd had hibernated all right, but they'd also done whatever it is that boy turtles and girl turtles do together, because there were all these baby turtles running around. I now had 42,000 turtles. I was worth $84,000! Why, I was making money faster than I could spend it.

We'd stay on the trail all spring and summer and fall, getting closer to Kansas City with each passing day. When winter came, I'd bury my herd. Then I'd dig them up each spring, and there'd always be more baby turtles...until finally, after five years, I had the largest herd the world has ever seen. I had a herd of 500,000 turtles. I was worth a million dollars.

All I had to do now was get them to Frenchy's Gourmet Eating Establishment and Pizza Parlor and collect my fortune. The only thing that stood between me and my million was the Big Muddy. It was a raging river, but I rode up and down until I found a gentle, shallow place to cross. I drove my herd in, and to my horror and surprise, they began to sink. You see, what no one had ever told me was that land turtles don't know how to swim.

But I'll tell you a secret. Every living thing will use the last ounce of its strength to survive. If you were to take a mouse and put it in a corner and then set a huge grizzly bear upon it, that mouse would stand up on its hind legs, ready to fight down to its last breath. It would do whatever it could to save its own life.

That's exactly what my turtles did.
They began paddling furiously,
trying to get across.

You should have seen them—
thousands and thousands
of little flippers
churning up the water like
tiny windmills.
It seemed as though
a blizzard was rising out
of that river.

And hours later, when all was calm again, there they were—my entire herd standing at the edge of Kansas City. Oh, I was proud.

Up Broadway we marched, heading directly for Frenchy's Gourmet Eating Establishment and Pizza Parlor. But what a shock when we arrived!

It was completely boarded up,
with a large sign that read:

CLOSED
Moved to
FRANCE

COME SEE
me in Paris
Frenchy

What to do? There was no other place to sell them.
The Atlantic Ocean seemed just a little too wide for
my turtles to swim across. Taking a boat wouldn't
work either—they'd all end up seasick. Obviously,
I couldn't let half a million turtles just wander
around the streets of Kansas City. There was
nothing else to do but lead them back to
Texas and let them go, which is exactly
what I did. And because we
already knew the way,
the journey wasn't
nearly as long.

So that's the true story of how I made and lost a
million dollars before I was old enough to vote.
No kidding.